C. White, A. White

A complete description of St. George's Cathedral

And hand-book to the Catholic antiquities of Southwark

C. White, A. White

A complete description of St. George's Cathedral
And hand-book to the Catholic antiquities of Southwark

ISBN/EAN: 9783741187681

Manufactured in Europe, USA, Canada, Australia, Japa

Cover: Foto ©Andreas Hilbeck / pixelio.de

Manufactured and distributed by brebook publishing software
(www.brebook.com)

C. White, A. White

A complete description of St. George's Cathedral

DESCRIPTION

OF

St. George's Cathedral.

Southwark in the Olden Time.

THE Borough of Southwark is situated on the southern bank of the Thames, opposite London. From the many Roman remains found near London-bridge, and in St. George's fields, there can be little doubt of the Romans having had a station here. After their departure, the Saxons availed themselves of the position, and from the name *South verk*, are supposed to have had some strong fortification here. William the Conqueror, enraged at the opposition he met with, laid Southwark in ashes. Of the remains of Catholic antiquity in Southwark, and indeed in all the metropolis, one of the most beautiful is the Church of *St. Mary Overies*, (over the *Rie* or water) near London Bridge. "This Church," writes Linstead, *its last prior*, "or some other in place thereof, was of old time, *long before the Conquest*, founded by a maiden named Mary, with a home for sisters. Unto the which house and sisters she left the oversight and profits of a cross ferry over the Thames, there kept before that any bridge was builded. This house of sisters was afterwards, by Swithin, a noble lady, converted into a College of priests, who, in place of the ferry, builded a bridge of timber," &c. * * * * * * * In the year 1106 was this Church again founded for canons regular, by William l'out de l'Arche, and William Dauncy, Kts.. Normans. Foundations, a part of this Church, which was burnt down in 1214, were discovered a few years ago. The present Church was rebuilt about 1400, and for this purpose Cardinal Beaufert, and John Gower the poet, (whose beautiful tomb, with its sweet and most Catholic inscription, may be seen in the south transept,) contributed largely.

Adjoining the Church were the residences of the Bishops of Winchester and Rochester, called *Winchester Hall* and *Rochester House*, the former being founded by Bishop Gifford in 1107, the latter about 1299.

The last grand Catholic function which took place in St. Mary's, was a solemn procession by command (it is said) of Henry VIII., when

> " Two and two they marched, and loud bells toll'd;
> One from a sprinkler holy water flung;
> This bore the relics in a chest of gold,
> On arm of that the swinging censer hung.
> The sweetest psalms of holy David sung
> ...   .
> And banners of the Church went waving in the wind."

And so at the first grand Catholic function in Southwark since that period, a most glorious procession took possession of the splendid Cathedral of which we are the humble chroniclers.

Sad is it to record, that the last prior of the house, *Linstead*, sold his holy office and religion to Henry VIII. for £100 a year.

And now let us see what this splendid building, the finest ancient Church in London after Westminster Abbey, was *some years ago*. It was a noble cruciform Church, 250 feet long, of the first and second styles of Pointed Architecture. The gem of the building is its exquisite altar screen, built by Bishop Fox. It is one mass of rich imagery work, similar to those in Winchester Cathedral, and St. Alban's Abbey Church. Can it be credited that it was decided by a majority of the inhabitants to *pull down* the lady chapel at the extreme east end, in order to effect some " improvements " (1) on the opening of new London Bridge ? Yet such was the case, and would have been carried into execution, had not some lovers of ancient art interfered, and obtained a reversal of the sentence. On which occasion subscriptions were raised, and the ancient structure was partly restored, though by the sacrifice of much that need not have been destroyed.* It is said that £80,000 have been expended on this structure during the present century.

An ancient Church dedicated to *St. Margaret* formerly stood on the site of the present Town Hall.

There was a Church dedicated to *St. George* in Southwark, in 1122. And hard by a village called *St. George's*, now part of the borough.

St. Thomas's Hospital was founded soon after the fire in 1214, " for converts and poor children," and called the Almery.

At *Bermondsey*, a religious house of the order of Cluny existed in 1089, and converted into an Abbey by Richard II. The parish Church was founded by the priors of this house, for the use of the inhabitants.

Another Church in Southwark, was dedicated to St. Olaf, or Olavo, the Danish Prince, massacred by his pagan subjects.

On *Sellenger's Wharf*, stood the town house of the Abbot of St. Augustine's at Canterbury.

The *Loke Hospital*, dedicated to St. Leonard, for leprous persons, existed in the time of Edward II.

In High Street there still exists the *Talbot* Inn, the Tabard of Chaucer's Canterbury pilgrims ; and not far west from St. Mary

---

* See on this subject the characteristic remarks of the tatented architect of St. George's Cathedral, in his second paper in the *Dublin Review*, " On the present state of Ecclesiastical Architecture in England."

Overies, stood the *Globe Theatre*, where the immortal bard of Avon first trod the stage.

Lambeth Palace.

The proximity of St. George's Cathedral to Lambeth Palace, the ancient town residence of the Archbishops of Canterbury, induces us to give some account of its foundation. A royal manor house existed in Lambeth in Saxon times, this fell to the see of Canterbury in 1197. The present palace was erected by Archbishop Boniface, in the second half of the thirteenth century. The present gateway, which for size and height, has, perhaps, no rival, was rebuilt about 1490 by Cardinal Morton. It would be no slight task to enumerate the great events which have taken place within these walls, the councils of prelates, the festivities at which kings and princes were guests, the royal marriages, the consecrations and other episcopal functions. Concerning one use the Catholic Archbishops of Canterbury made of their wealth, Godwin tells us of Archbishop Winchelsea, that he gave alms to five thousand poor a year at the palace gate, and sent meat and drink to such as were unable to attend, and that he had particular compassion on such as had fallen from wealth to poor estate, &c.

The Great Hall, the Chapel, (though much defaced, and filled with Protestant furniture,) the Guard Room, and a few other smaller apartments, are all that remain of the ancient palace. The new buildings were lately erected, and though the exterior presents a pleasing and correct adaptation of the Tudor; the interior courts are quite in the modern style.

Among the portraits which adorn the palace, the one most striking to a Catholic visitor is the mild and thoughtful figure of the last Archbishop of Canterbury, Cardinal Pole. It is a copy, and a very faithful one, of the portrait in the Barberini palace at Rome.

It is rather a singular coincidence, that the last Primate of the Catholic Church in England, and our first Metropolitan, Archbishop of Westminster, should be Cardinals of Holy Church.

The Gordon Riots.

Passing to modern times, it is recorded that "on the 2nd of June, 1780, sixty thousand rioters and lawless men assembled in St. George's Fields. They were drawn up in martial array, with flags and streamers, on which were emblazoned the fiercest denunciations of the Catholic faith. Their object was to destroy that faith by force of arms, and to reduce to ashes the chapels and dwellings of the Catholics in the metropolis. Led on by Lord George Gordon, who harangued them with the most inflammatory language, and painted every horror which a diseased imagination or the insanity which lurked in his constitution could devise, about the practices and doctrines of Catholicity; he exasperated to madness the passions of his hearers, and then marched at their head to commence the work of pillage and conflagration. On the very spot where Lord George Gordon preached his wild crusade against Catholicity, St. George's Cathedral now stands! Here, where the downfal and total annihilation of the Catholic faith in England was vainly imagined, within the space of a man's life we behold the seat of the Cardinal Archbishop of Westminster, the first metropolitan of the restored Catholic Hierarchy in this country, "Lauda Jerusalem Dominum, *quia* non fecit taliter omni nationi." Ps. cxlvii. Praise the Lòrd, O Jerusalem : *for* He hath not done in like manner to every nation.

The Catholic Mission in Southwark.

There are perhaps few remaining who remember the time when the holy sacrifice of the Mass was offered up in secret chambers, at whose doors stood faithful sentinels, who, scrutinizing the features of every new comer, gave admission only to such as were well known to be of the household of the faith.

About 1788 " a house was taken, and a room opened, which was by some judged sufficiently large for the purpose." This was situated in Bandy-leg Walk, near Guildford Street. "But," continues the address from the Committee for the erection of a chapel for the inhabitants of the Borough, Southwark, Lambeth, Newington, Walworth, and other adjacent villages, " but it was soon found that it would not contain one-half of the congregation ; and that it was in other respects very unfit, both on account of its situation and ruinous condition. Notwithstanding these disadvantages, the great good that visibly appeared from this feeble essay, convinced all who were witnesses of it, that it was a duty they owed to God and their neighbour, to use their utmost endeavours to carry, if possible, a plan of erecting a chapel into immediate execution. Hence earnest application was made to the late Bishop Talbot, who approved of the undertaking." A site was procured in the London Road, and plans on the most economical principle were furnished by the late Mr. Taylor, of Weybridge. Much opposition was however experienced from some timid persons, who thought the size of the chapel too large, and of cathedral like appearance ! The execution of the plan was delayed some months, at the suggestion of the Catholic Committee. But towards the close of the year 1789, having £500 in hand, and the estimate for the buildings being £2,000, the chapel was commenced, and roofed in before the following winter. The chapel was opened to public worship by Bishop Douglass, on Passion Sunday, (it being St. Patrick's day,) 1793, and the dedication sermon was preached by the celebrated Father O'Leary. The clergy whose names are attached to the above-named address, are the Revs. Messrs. Lindow, Lucas, Griffiths, and Varley.

This mission has been served by the following priests. The Revs. Thos. White, 1791, afterwards of Winchester, and author of a volume of sermons ; Peter Collingridge, O. S. F., 1791, afterwards Bishop in the Western district ; Thouse Stout, 1795 ; Joseph Hodgson, 1795, afterwards V. G. to Bishop Douglass ; John Singleton, 1802, who left for the Northern mission ; James Bramston, 1801, afterwards in 1823 Bishop in the London district ; Thomas Pitchford, 1801 ; Daniel

McDonnell, O. S. F., 1811, afterwards in 1829 Bishop of Trinidad ⁚ Charles McDonnell, O. S. F., his brother, 1815; *Thomas Doyle*, Sept. 1820; John Kearns, 1823, now at Brockhampton Havant; *John Radford*, 1824, deceased in 1812; *John White*, 1829, dec. in 1842; Bernard Jarrett, now S. J.; Matthew Ryan, 1838, since retired to the Cistercians; *Edward McStay*, 1839, dec. 1812; John Telford, 1840, now at Ryde; *Jeremiah Cotter*, 1842; George Rolfe, 1843, now at Moorfields; Peter Kaye, 1844, now at Blackburn; Thomas Richardson, 1845, now at East Hendred; Ignatius Collingridge, 1845, now at Winchester; *James Danell*, 1846; George Talbot, 1847, now Private Chaplain to His Holiness Pius IX.

On the opening of the new Church the clergy attached to it were the Revs. T. Doyle, D.D., J. Cotter, J. Danell, G. Talbot, J. Wheble, and F. Oakeley. The last three have retired, the first to Rome, the second to Chelsea, and the third to Islington; and the Rev. J. G. Wenham, late Protestant Chaplain to the troops at Ceylon, is now the fourth priest. *Floreant.*

In 1850, on the feast of St. Michael, September 29th, His Holiness Pope Pius IX. signed an apostolic letter, by which he suppressed the Vicarial powers of our Bishops, and restored to England her Hierarchy, appointing a Metropolitan see of Westminster, and twelve suffragan Bishoprics. Of these, one of the most important, from its position and the extent of its territory, is the diocese of Southwark, which comprises the counties of Surrey, Sussex, Kent, Berkshire, Hampshire, and the channel Islands. In consequence of this arrangement, St. George's became a Cathedral Church, and His Eminence the Cardinal Archbishop of Westminster being appointed Bishop (Administrator) of the See of Southwark, this Cathedral is used by his Eminence as the temporary seat of his Metropolitan see, of which he took possession on the feast of St. Nicholas, 6 Dec. 1850.

The baptismal registers of St. George commence in the year 1788. In 1789 the number of entries were 75. In 1843 their number was 785. In 1829 the present diocese of Southwark contained 32 chapels, served by 33 priests. In the present year 1851 there are 58 churches and chapels, served by 70 priests; one religious house of men, and 9 convents, one of which is at present the old chapel in the London Road, occupied by the Benedictine Solitaries of the perpetual Adoration, devoted to the discharge of the united duties of Martha and Mary.

𝕿𝖍𝖊 𝕰𝖗𝖊𝖈𝖙𝖎𝖔𝖓 𝖔𝖋 𝕾𝖙. 𝕲𝖊𝖔𝖗𝖌𝖊'𝖘.

In the course of nearly half a century after its erection, the chapel in the London Road being found totally inadequate to the accommodation of the increasing congregation who might be seen on Sundays not only filling it, but even the hall and a great portion of the adjoining entrance court, it was determined to erect a new church. Accordingly a site was sought, and some improvements having taken place in St. George's Fields, by enclosing the space opposite Bethlehem Hospital, and continuing St. George's Road into the Westminster Road, a piece of ground having a frontage in the former road of 500 feet, and of nearly 100 in the Lambeth and Westminster Roads, was bought of the Bridge House Estate, for £3,200, in 1839. Designs were furnished by Augustus Welby Pugin, Esq., a recent convert to our Holy Faith, and as in the case of the chapel in the London Road, many protested against the erection of so vast a church as most extravagant and unnecessary, and not likely to be filled, and many other of those objections which the timid ever produce against any grand and bold design. The plan was, however, eventually accepted. And here we must say, - in justice to the Architect, that his design was for a *parish* church, and that he had no idea that it would eventually be erected into a *cathedral* church. He was also very much tied by the stringent instructions of the Committee to provide for 3,000 worshippers on the floor of the building, and to make the church as ornate as possible. This of course obliged him to sacrifice many noble features of so large a church, as clerestory, &c., and to contract the dimensions of the chancel and chapels. But there are several existing specimens of ancient churches of large dimensions, such as those of Grantham and Great Yarmouth, which have no clerestories.

This plan was adopted, and the ground having been enclosed, the foundations were commenced on the Feast of the Nativity of our Blessed Lady, (Sept. 8th), 1840, and the foundation stone was laid by the Rev. J. White, in the absence of Dr. Doyle, on the Feast of St. Augustine, the Apostle of England, (May 26,) in the following year.

The Dedication.

This solemn ceremony took place on the 4th of July, it being the (transferred) Feast of St. Alban, Proto-Martyr of England, in the year 1848. Three thousands persons, including many of the Catholic aristocracy, and other distinguished members of the Church, and many Protestants, filled the vast nave and aisles long before the appointed time for the commencement of the service. A little after eleven, the procession began to move from the sacristy, down the cloister, and outside the church to the grand entrance, in the following order :—Thurifer, cross-bearer, and acolyths, choir-boys and choristers, two-and-two. The secular clergy, about 230, two abreast. The religious orders in their respective costumes. The Institute of Charity, the Redemptorists, the Passionists, the Jesuits, the Franciscans, the Dominicans, the Cistercians, the Benedictines, &c. The Foreign Clergy and Canons. Then followed the Bishops, each attended by his chaplain and trainbearer, and vested in cope and mitre. The Right Revs., Bishops Davis, of Maitland, Morris, Gillis, Ullathorne, Sharples, Brown of Wales, Wareing, Brown of Lancashire, Briggs. The Bishops of Elphin, Tournai, Liege, Treves and Luxembourg. Book, and Bugie Bearers. Mitre and Crosier Bearers. The Deacon and Subdeacon of the Mass. The Assistant Priest. The Bishop's Deacons. The Right Rev. Nicholas Wiseman, D.D., Pro. V.A. of the London District, (now Cardinal Archbishop of Westminster.) Trainbearer, &c., &c.

Such was the long, stately, and heart-cheering procession, the like of which had not been seen in England for three centuries. "Three hundred ecclesiastics of almost every rank, from the right reverend Bishop to the humble acolyte and the innocent child who hold the celebrant's train ; mitres and crosiers, rich copes and the black serge of the Passionists, with the white habits of the Cistercians, and the long array of surpliced priests, presented a *coup d'œil* which seems to . have struck every beholder, of whatever creed or opinion, with a religious awe, and which will never depart from their memory."

The Procession, consisting of about 300 persons, moved with solemnity up the nave, the choir singing the "Hæc dies." On reaching the upper portion of the nave, the clergy and assistants ranged themselves on either side, and allowed the Bishops and their chaplains, who with the officiating Bishop and clergy, were the only persons admitted within the chancel.

High Mass was sung by Bishop Wiseman, who after the Gospel, mounted the pulpit and preached (his deacons standing behind him bearing his mitre and crosier) from the 117th Psalm, "The Lord is God, and hath shone upon us......Thou art my God, and I will praise Thee ; Thou art my God, and I will exalt Thee."

In the course of a sermon full of joyful exultation at the mercies of God on this country, the Bishop read an affecting letter he had received from the late Archbishop of Paris, regretting his inability to attend the function, but promising his prayers for those present. His Grace had been sacrificed as a victim for his distracted country, a few days after writing that, one of his last letters.

The High Mass then proceeded, and the procession returned to the sacristy in the same order it had entered the church.

At half-past four, vespers were chaunted, and a most impressive discourse was preached by Bishop Gillis of Edinburgh, on the text, "All power is given to me in heaven and on earth, go ye therefore and teach all nations." At the conclusion of which, his Lordship addressed a few words in French, with perfect ease and fluency, to the foreign Bishops, thanking them for their kindness in coming over to assist at this solemn dedication of the largest and most splendid temple erected in England, for the Catholic Church, since the schism of the sixteenth century.

An Octave of services followed the opening, at which sermons were preached by the following clergymen :—The Bishop of Liege, Bishop Wiseman, Bishop Morris, Bishop Brown of Wales, the Rev. F. Oakeley, Father Ignatius, (Hon. and Rev. G. Spencer,) Passionist, Father Petcherine, Redemptorist, and Fathers Faber and Dalgairns, Oratorians. On the Saturday after the opening, a solemn dirge was sung for the repose of the soul of the Hon. Edward Petre, by Dr. Doyle, and a funeral oration delivered by Bishop Morris; Bishop Wiseman and four other Bishops attending, and pronouncing the absolution.

And now that the glorious work is accomplished, of raising in the metropolis of England the largest church dedicated to the worship of the Almighty in this country since she fell into schism, it remains to

say a few words as to the way in which it has been accomplished.
The chief instrument in its erection, under Divine Providence, has
been the Very Rev. Thomas Doyle, D.D., who through the space of
ten long laborious years, in spite of the greatest difficulties and obsta-
cles in his way, devoted himself most generously to the great work ;
making many journies through England and a great part of Europe to
solicit the alms of the faithful, and obtaining strength and encourage-
ment at the shrine of the Apostles, to persevere in its accomplish-
ment. Nobly were his efforts seconded by his reverend confreres, and
the much respected secretary to the church, M. Forristall, Esq., and
other lay members of the congregation, amongst whom the names of
Mausse, Knill, Hodges, and Ernest Scott, Esqs., are conspicuous. And
most generously and perseveringly did the subscriptions of the congregation pour in, in aid of the work, and proud may they be of now pos-
sessing a most glorious church which has already been, and is doubtless
destined, in God's Providence, to exercise an important influence in
drawing the attention of our separated countrymen to the beauties and
grandour of the external worship of God's Holy Church. *Fiat, fiat.*

DESCRIPTION OF THE CATHEDRAL.

The Plan.

T GEORGE's CATHEDRAL * consists of a nave, having a Tower at one extremity, and a chancel
at the other ; and aisles terminated by chapels.

St. George the Martyr has ever been held in great ven-
eration by the Christian world, and he is known to a large
portion of it by the name of the *Great Martyr.*
The early writers bear testimony to the fervour with
which he was invoked previous to battles, the fate
of which was often attributed to his miraculous in-
tervention. Thus he is said to have appeared to
Richard, the lion hearted King of England, when
engaged with the Saracens, and this vision so encour-
aged the English troops, that they won the victory. These
and other favours so increased the devotion of the English to
St. George, that at the great National Council held at Oxford
in 1222, he was invoked as the protector and Patron of England, and his festival, April 23rd, ordered to be kept as a holyday of
the first rank in this country. Under his name and ensign was
instituted, by our victorious king, Edward III., in 1350, the most
noble Order of the Garter, the chief military order in Europe, consisting of twenty five knights, beside the sovereign. Many other distinguished orders also claim St. George for their patron. Portugal, Arragon, Genoa,
and other countries revere him as their tutelar saint.
The most authentic acts of his martyrdom relate that he lived in the early part of
the fourth century. He was a native of Cappadocia, his parents being noble Christians. He embraced the profession of a soldier, and served with much distinction in
the Roman army. But when the Emperor Dioclesian commenced his persecution of
the Christians, St. George threw up his commission and posts, and complained to the
Emperor of his bloody edicts. He was immediately cast into prison, and tried, first
by promises, and afterwards put to the question, and tortured with great cruelty ;

Its internal length is 240 feet by 70. The material employed in its construction is a hard yellow brick, and Caen stone for the ornamental parts. The builder employed to carry out Mr. Pugin's designs, was Mr. Meyers. The style of the Church is decorated or middle pointed, of the time of Edward III., having geometric tracery in the windows. Some have imagined that it resembles the ancient church of the Austin Friars in the city. It contains 14 pillars, 49 windows having 154 lights, 3 principal and 21 small doorways. The total cost of the Cathedral, with Bishop's and Clergy's residence, in their present state, has been £30,000. Of this sum there still remains a few thousands to be paid, which it is confidently hoped will soon be generously contributed by some zealous Catholics, and thus put it in the power of Dr. Doyle to petition for its consecration.*

* There are alms-boxes and others for special purposes in various parts of the Church. Bequests to the Cathedral should be made to the Trustees of the Roman Catholic Church of St. George, St. George's Road, Southwark, in the County of Surrey.

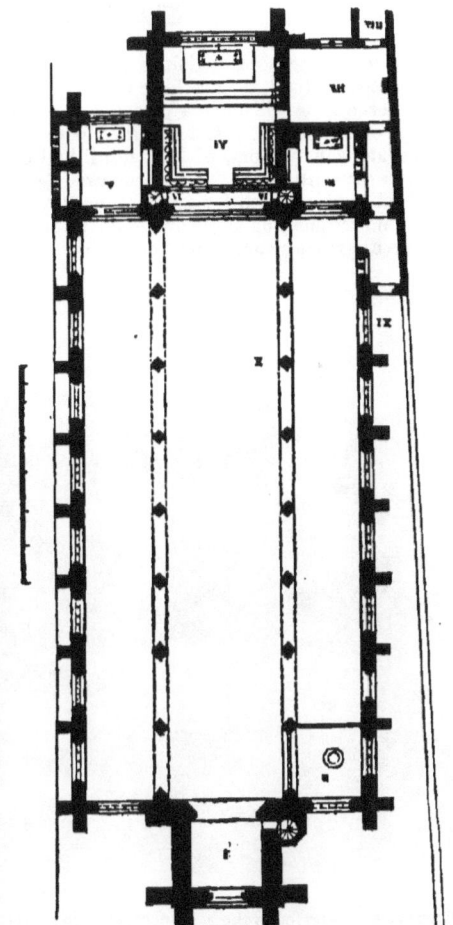

I. Tower.
II. Font.
III. Chapel of the B. Virgin.
IV. Chancel.
V. Chapel of the B. Sacrament.
VI. Staircase to rood loft.
VII. Sacristy.
VIII. Cloister leading to Priest's house.
IX. Petre chantry.
X. Pulpit.

but nothing could shake his constancy. The next day he was led through the city and beheaded. Such seems to be the groundwork of the innumerable Greek and Latin legends of the life of this illustrious martyr of Christ, in whose honour more

The Exterior.

Wo will imagino tho visitor to approach the Cathodral from tho Westminster Road, on reaching the bond which brings him in sight of St. Goorge's, he will have a pleasing group before him of the dwelling-houses of tho clergy. The building, with the pretty little oriel window chapel and school-room, with its spiral bell turret, was originally design-ed for a convent, but has never been used for that purpose, but will in all probability be adapted for a palace for the Bishop of Southwark. The erection occupies the angle of tho St. George's and Westminster Roads.

Our Engraving shews the houses and the many gabled chancel end

churches were erected in the early ages than to any other saint beside the Blessed Virgin and the Apostles.

It is supposed that the legend of his combat with the dragon arose in the East, sometime in the eleventh century, and that it was brought into Europe by the cru-saders, in whose ranks it is said St. George was often seen fighting against the Sara-cens. The banner of the saint, known over the world as St. George's flag, is a Greek cross of a bright red colour on a white ground, though some ancient flags bore a representation of the Saint trampling on the dragon. This latter representation is the one adopted in our mediæval churches, in sculpture, painted glass, and other embellishments. The Church, in adopting this mode of figuring the Saint, would teach us the victory which the saints and every Christian gains over the demon, in overcoming the temptations to which he is subjected ; it is also a fit emblem of the constant warfare which the Church of God is ever waging against the world, and of her delivery of her children from its hostile attacks.—See *Butler's Lives of the Saints,* vol. iv., April 23.

ST. GEORGE'S CATHEDRAL IN ITS PRESENT STATE

-of the Cathedral, with its elegant turrets.   Passing down St. George's Road, we will pause to admire the side of the Cathedral, with its rich pinnacles, open parapet, and magnificent five light decorated windows of varied design.   Under the parapet the following legend is carved in ancient characters ; *This Church, dedicated in honor of Saint George the Martyr, was erected in the year* 1848.

The Tower and Great Entrance.

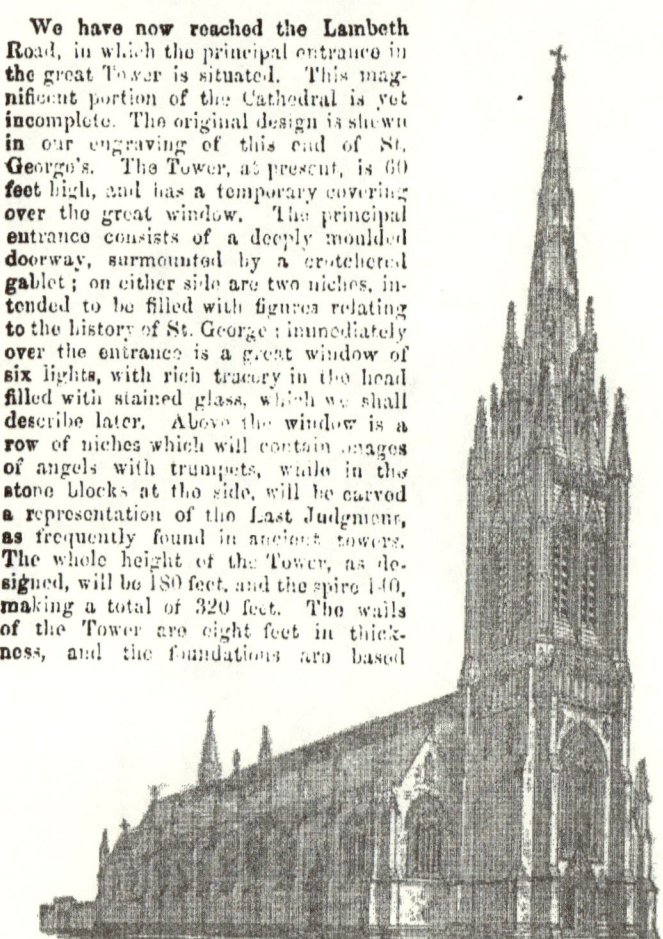

We have now reached the Lambeth Road, in which the principal entrance in the great Tower is situated.   This magnificent portion of the Cathedral is yet incomplete. The original design is shewn in our engraving of this end of St. George's.   The Tower, at present, is 60 feet high, and has a temporary covering over the great window.   The principal entrance consists of a deeply moulded doorway, surmounted by a crotcheted gablet ; on either side are two niches, intended to be filled with figures relating to the history of St. George : immediately over the entrance is a great window of six lights, with rich tracery in the head filled with stained glass, which we shall describe later.   Above the window is a row of niches which will contain images of angels with trumpets, while in the stone blocks at the side, will be carved a representation of the Last Judgment, as frequently found in ancient towers. The whole height of the Tower, as designed, will be 180 feet, and the spire 140, making a total of 320 feet.   The walls of the Tower are eight feet in thickness, and the foundations are based

Interior from the B. Secrament Aisle.

C. WHITE & THOS TURNER DELT ET LITHᴱ

PRINTED BY T. TURNER GRAVE CT FLEET S.

on a solid mass of concrete, capable of bearing any pressure that may be laid on it.

The Interior.

We will now conduct the visitor over the interior of the sacred edifice, premising that the Blessed Sacrament is continually reserved on one of its altars, so that the Catholic visitor will spend some moments in adoration on entering, and we would remind others of the sacred character of the building, and request them to observe the regulations for visitors which are posted at the entrance.

The Cathedral not being built to the East, we will speak of the right and left aisles, supposing the visitor to be facing the Chancel, the latter is called the " Blessed Sacrament aisle," the former " Our Lady's aisle."

On either side, in the interior of the Tower, are holy water stoups, and on the right a doorway leading to the organ gallery and tower. On the left will be seen placed on a triptie, the mortuary list of Catholics lately deceased, for whom the prayers of the faithful are requested. A little in advance is a large font-like alms box for the poor. The organ * is placed in the Tower in a loft composed of solid carpentry, with clamped beams and carved enrichments. A great arch eleven feet thick and forty high, opens the Tower to the nave. Our view of the interior is taken from the B. Sacrament aisle.

The Font.

On the right, in the last bay of our Lady's aisle, is the Font, which is raised on an octagon platform of stone, ascended by steps on four sides and enclosed with a brass railing. The Font is octagonal, eight angels spring from the angles of the shaft, and support the bowl, divided by pinnacled buttresses into eight compartments, containing images of the four Evangelists, and the four principal Doctors of the Church.

* Compass of Great and Choir Organs, GG to F in alt. *Great Organ* contains :— 1—Open diapason, metal through; 2—Open diapason; 3—Stopped diapason; 4—Principal, large scale; 5—Principal, small ditto; 6—12th; 7—15th; 8—Sesquialtra ; 9—Mixture; 10—Trumpet treble; 11—Trumpet bass; 12—Clarion; 13—Pedal pipes from GGG.

Choir Organ. 1—Stopped diapason bass; 2—Claribella treble; 3—Dulceana; 4 - Principal; 5—Flute; 6—Fifteenth; 7—Keraulophon; 8—Cremona.

Compass of Swell, from Gamut G to F in alt., containing : 1—Open diapason; 2—Stopped diapason; 3—Principal; 4—15th; 5—Sesquialtra; 6—Trumpet; 7—Hautboy; 8—Clarion.

Couplers. Great to Pedals; Choir to Pedals; Swell to Great.

3 Composition Pedals to Great Organ; 2 ditto ditto to Choir Organ; 2 ditto ditto to Swell.

An octave and half of German Pedals.

There is a long movement which brings the performer some feet in the front of the Organ. Built by Bishop and Son, Lisson Grove.

This beautiful Font sadly lacks one of those lofty spiral covers which yet remain in many of the ancient churches of England. The baptistry is enclosed by a low open screen.

The Pulpit,

Is seen on proceeding up the nave, attached to the third pillar from the chancel. It has been designed from some of the finest early Italian examples, as at Pisa and Pistoia. The form is hexagonal, supported by marble shafts, the centre one resting on a base sculptured with the emblems of the four Evangelists. On four sides of the body of the pulpit are *bassi relievi*, most exquisitely carved, representing our Lord preaching the Sermon on the Mount, St. John the Baptist preaching in the Wilderness, and the preaching of the religious orders represented by St. Francis and St. Dominic. These sculptures are executed with the severity of the early Florentine school, and many of the figures are studies from nature and real drapery. The ascent to the Pulpit is by a series of detached steps, each supported by marble shafts and richly carved capitals, to which is attached a wrought iron railing of elaborate design. This work is entirely

executed of Caen stone, and the shafts are worked in British marble. There is a temporary sounding board, which it is to be hoped will soon be replaced by a work in accordance with the beauty of the pulpit.

We will now turn to the tower end, and shall have a good view of the great window with its beautiful painted glass, containing figures of SS. George Martyr, Richard, Ethelbert, Oswald, Edmund, and Edward the Confessor, with angels bearing scrolls and instruments. Again, facing the chancel, we have before us

The Rood Screen,

which divides the chancel from the nave. It is a double screen of stone, supporting a rood loft. This ancient, symbolical, and beautiful, division of that portion of the Church intended for the faithful, from that appointed to the Clergy, and those assisting in the celebration of the sacred rites, has been revived in all its glory. The front is composed of three open arches, resting on marble shafts, with richly carved foliated caps, surmounted by a string course, with carved bosses and angels, supporting an open parapet. The back is likewise composed of three arches, the centre serving for the doorway, (which has gates of wrought iron,) and two others filled with light open tracery, and oak ribbed ceiling, is fixed between the two screens, and immediately over is the loft on which is fixed the great rood. This cross, an original work of the fifteenth century, was purchased in Belgium, and restored to its present beauty : it is one of the finest examples existing, quite equal to that of Louvain, and probably executed by the same artist. The image of our Lord, is by the chisel of the celebrated M. Durlet, of Antwerp, the architect of the new stalls in the Cathedral of that city. The images of our Blessed Lady, and St. John, were carved in England. The gilding and painting on this cross are restorations of the original decoration, ample traces of which remained on the carving. The loft is ascended by two staircases, which are terminated, by pinnacled, and crocketed turrets, in which are hung the Sanctus and Angelus bells. On great festivals the loft is filled with lights, and decorated with flowers and shrubs.

The Chancel,

Is forty feet long, and about the same in height ; the space between the screen and sanctuary is panelled with oak tracery, and fitted with seats and richly carved desks of the same material, capable of seating forty persons. Crocketed arches, springing from shafts resting on a stone seat, are built round the sanctuary ; three of these (on the right hand side), deeper than the rest, serve for the sedilia, or seats of the officiating clergy, and contain appropriate emblems for priest, deacon, and subdeacon ; the remainder are intended for the assistants. The floor is laid with encaustic tiles. The ceiling is divided into three compartments by carved principals resting on angel corbels ; each compartment is subdivided by moulded ribs into square panels, which are intended to be enriched by painting on a gold ground. The great window of nine lights is filled with stained glass, representing the root of Jesse, or genealogy of our Lord. This was the gift of the Earl of Shrewsbury. The three side windows contain figures of St. George the martyr, patron of the cathedral ; St. Stephen, deacon, the first martyr; and St. Lawrence, deacon and martyr. The large window is by *Wailes*, and the side ones by *Hardman*. A temporary episcopal throne is erected opposite the sedilia, and is used by the bishop and his deacons.

The High Altar.

St. Georges.

The High Altar

Is composed of Caen stone, surmounted by a slab of marble; the front is divided into three quatrefoils filled with bass reliefs, representing the Transfiguration, Resurrection, and Ascension of our Lord. In the centre of the altar is placed the tabernacle, worked in Caen stone; it consists of four clusters of pinnacles, supporting a richly crocketed canopy, surmounted by another containing a pelican, as an emblem of our Redeemer shedding his blood for man. The whole is richly gilt and painted, and the doors of the tabernacle are of metal chased with gilt, and enriched with large crystals. Immediately behind the altar is an elaborately carved stone reredos or back, composed of ten small, and two large niches, filled with images of angels bearing emblems, and Saints Peter and Paul. The figure of the crucifix is of ivory most exquisitely carved, and partly coloured from nature.

All the furniture of the high altar and sanctuary has been designed in strict accordance with the building. Two high standing candelabra of brass supporting coronal lights, are placed on either side of the altar, on stone pedestals. Six large candlesticks of brass of hexagonal form resting on lions, stand on the altar steps, with numerous smaller candlesticks and branches, and vessels for flowers, &c. A lamp and coronal for six lights is suspended in front of the altar, and two smaller ones on either side. Lower in the chancel hangs a large corona of iron, most artificially wrought, painted, and gilt, with brass enrichments, shields, inscriptions, and crystal knobs; it is composed of two circles in the height, and will carry from fifty to sixty tapers.

Below is a most rich brass eagle or lectern, made up of wrought metal, consisting of many pieces, and having two large branches for lights. It contains nine hundred pounds weight of brass, and was presented to the church by the Rev. Daniel Haigh of Erdington.

Chapel of the Blessed Sacrament.

On the left of the chancel is the chapel of the most Blessed Sacrament, divided off from the aisle by a high and richly wrought iron screen, enriched with lambs and chalices alternate in brass. The upper part of this screen forms a cresting, with candlesticks for lights. The floor is laid with encaustic tiles of various colours, representing lambs, crosses, and other appropriate devices. The walls and ceiling are entirely covered with painted decorations; the ribs of the ceiling are gold, with red panels, relieved with cherubim, vine leaves, and grapes.

The walls are covered with diapered work interspersed with angels, bearing scrolls on gilt grounds. The passion flower is introduced in the borders and divisions of the quatrefoils.

The altar is supported by four cherubim attached to pillars. In the centre panel is the Agnus Dei, with four angels incensing, and two cherubim in the side panels. The altar is surmounted by a

2

reredos and tabernacle of rich design, carved in Caen stone ; the two
largor quatrefoils are filled by bas reliefs of the offering of Melchise-
dec, and the Jews gathering manna in the desert ; the other panels
contain cherubim and vine foliage. Two curtains of rich stuff are
suspended by iron brackets on either side of the altar ; these brackets
or rods are very highly wrought ; in each is an inscription in perfora-
ted brass : " Adoremus in eternum Sanctissimum Sacramentum,"—
" Let us adore for ever the most Holy Sacrament." A bratishing
of trefoil work runs along the top of the rod, which is terminated by a
standard for lights. In front of the altar is hung a silver coronal and
lamp ; the coronal is hexagonal in form, and inscribed with the six
attributes of God, and other inscriptions. The window over the altar
contains a figure of our Lord, surrounded by cherubim, and the side
ones are composed of quatrefoil patterns, filled with angels bearing
scrolls. In the recess below are four small lights, containing figures
of St. Charles Borromeo, Bishop of Milan, St. Alban, Proto-martyr of
England, St. Thomas of Canterbury, and St. John the Evangelist.
     Again passing the chancel, we reach the

Chapel of the Blessed Virgin,

Which is also richly painted and gilt ; only here the symbolical
colour of blue is chiefly prominent. . The ribs of the ceiling are gilt,
with blue panels, containing our Lady's monogram, surrounded by
white roses and stars. The walls are diapered in blue, with gilt
fleurs-de lis.
     The altar is divided into three compartments, separated by angels
in small canopied niches ; the centre division contains the pot of
lilies, with our Lady and the angel Gabriel on either side ; the reredos
is surmounted by a row of niches and tabernacle work, with an image
of the Blessed Virgin and angels holding lights ; the two end clusters
of pinnacles run up on each side of the window, and are terminated by
images of angels. The window over the altar contains, in the centre
light, a figure of our Blessed Lady, with angels ; the side windows
contain the Annunciation and Presentation.
     The altar plate is of metal silvered parcel, gilt and enamelled,
exceedingly rich and beautiful. Before the altar hangs a circular
silvered lamp, richly worked with fleur-de-lis and stars. This lamp
sheds a continual blue light over our Lady's sanctuary.
     This chapel is divided from the church by a carved oak screen,
surmounted by a row of candlesticks.
     On a richly carved corbel, between this chapel and the chancel, is a
large figure of the Blessed Virgin, richly gilt and drapered, before
which a small silver lamp is suspended. On her festivals, this statue
is decorated with lights and flowers.
     Returning down our Lady's aisle, in the second bay from the
chapel, we see

Drawn by C White   Daniel Grant & Co Litho

The Petre Chantry
St George's

The Petre Chantry,

Founded for the repose of the soul of the late Hon. Edward Petre, of Selby, in Yorkshire, and endeared to the memory of the London Catholics, for his long connexion with, and strenuous advocacy of, their charities, and for his zealous efforts in the cause of the education of poor Catholic children.

The chantry is a most chaste and beautiful erection in the perpendicular style of architecture, opening into the aisle by a low archway, under which stands the tomb of Caen stone, covered with a slab of black marble inlaid with a brass cross, fleury enamelled, and circular emblems of the evangelists in the corners. At the foot of the cross is the following inscription : " Credo quod Redemptor meus vivit, et in novissimo die de terra surrecturus sum et in carne mea videbo Deum salvatorem meum."—" I believe that my Redeemer liveth, and that I shall arise from the earth on the last day, and see in my flesh God my Saviour."

Round the slab are read the following words : " Of your charity pray for the soul of the Honourable Edward Petre, who departed this life on the 8th day of June, in the year of our Lord, 1848, aged 54 years."

On the sides of the tomb are shields on which the arms of Petre and Stafford are enamelled, and it is surrounded by a wrought iron railing, painted and gilt, with standards bearing the Petre arms. Attached to the centre rails is a brass scroll, calling upon the faithful to " pray for the soul of Edward Petre," with which pious request we trust every reader will devoutly comply.

The chantry is entered by a small doorway, containing a richly carved oak door. Its dimensions are sixteen feet by five and a half, and eleven feet high. In the centre a large stone slab with rings, covers the vault to which the body of the deceased was transferred from its temporary resting place in the old chapel in the London Road, on the completion of the chantry in 1849.

The chantry is built entirely of stone, the sides of tracered panels, and the roof of fan groining, in the bosses of which are the monograms of our Blessed Lady, and of the late Hon. E. Petre, and his amiable lady ; over the tomb on the left side, the family motto : " Sans Dieu rien,"—" No good but from God," is painted in ancient letters.

The altar is privileged. It is of very small dimensions ; its front is carved with a figure of our Blessed Lady and her Divine Son, seated with attendant angels bearing lights. The reredos is composed of three compartments, which are most exquisitely carved in stone ; the centre one represents our Saviour on the cross attended by our Blessed Lady, St. John, and Mary Magdalen. The compartment on the left contains figures of the Hon. E. Petre, kneeling with his patron, St. Edward the Confessor, and angels ; that on the right the Hon. Mrs. Petre, with her patron, St. Lawrence the Deacon, and angels. The whole painted and partly gilt. The altar is supplied with every requisite for the celebration of low masses. The stained glass, beau-

tifully executed by Hardman, fills three twolight windows, which contain
figures of St. George the martyr, our Blessed Lady, St. Edward the
Confessor, St. Lawrence, deacon, St. Robert, abbot, and St. Germanus,
bishop.   Mass is daily offered up for the repose of the soul of the founder,
and all christian souls.

This is the only chantry at present in the cathedral ; but we hear
that one or two others are in contemplation.

Next to the Petre chantry is one of

The Confessionals,

Which are built between the buttresses, and divided into three
closets, the centre one being occupied by the priest, the side ones in
turn by the penitents.   They are entered by plain door-ways ; the heads
of which are exquisitely carved in open stone work, the centre having
emblems of the purity and sanctity of the priestly character, and the
power of the keys ; the sides, the discipline, and other emblems of
penance and mortification.   The confessionals receive light through
small circular windows at the back.

At the end of the Blessed Sacrament aisle, stands a large bronze crucifix.   This splendid work is said to be from a design by Michael Angelo,
and was much admired by Canova.   It was some time in Napoleon's
favourite chateau at Malmaison, near Paris.   The figure is larger than
life size, and the cross and stand is near eleven feet high.   We see a
subscription is on foot to obtain a canopy and lamp for it.   Might we
suggest the formation of a Calvary chapel, so common abroad, with
corresponding figures of our Blessed Lady, St. John, and Mary
Magdalen ?

The windows of the aisles will be eventually filled with stained glass.
Two already have figures in their central lights, of St. Patrick, Apostle
and first Primate of Ireland, and of St. Vincent of Paul, the Apostle
of Charity in the seventeenth century.   Others of St. Dominic and the
Rosary are, we hear, in preparation.

Between the pillars of the Nave are brass standards for four jets of
gas each, and the Cathedral is warmed by hot air, generated by gas
apparatus placed at intervals in the aisles.

Near the Lady Chapel a doorway leads the visiter into a cloister, at the end of which is the sacristy, a fine apartment, 29 feet by 22½, having an open wooden roof, and containing various closets, ambries, and chests for the vestments, and church furniture. Among the most remarkable pieces of Church plate, are a splendid chalice of solid gold, having the arms of the present Pope on the foot. It was presented to the Church by His Holiness Pope Pius IX., as a testimony of his good feeling to the English Catholics, and his satisfaction at the dedication of St. George's; a beautiful gold and silver gilt monstrance of ancient form, set with stones; a silver chalice, exquisitely chased and enamelled; a silver ciborium most beautifully wrought; a processional cross, covered with gilt metal plates of raised work, and set with enamels and crystals; and several other beautiful specimens of the goldsmith's craft. Besides an immense assortment of candlesticks and branches, by which the chancel may be lit on great festivals with many hundred lights. All the metal work in the Cathedral is from Mr. Hardman's manufactory at Birmingham.

The vestments, of which there are several handsome sets, were made by Mrs. Powell and daughters, of the same town.

In the wardrobe are cassocks and surplices for about thirty children and about fifty men, who assist at the great functions of the Church.

The Confraternities.

Attached to this Cathedral are the following Confraternities or religious brotherhoods. The holy Guild of St. George the Martyr. The Confraternities of the Most Blessed Sacrament; of the Sacred Heart of Jesus; of the Passion of our Lord; of the Scapular; of the Rosary; of the Immaculate Heart of Mary for the Conversion of Sinners; of Prayers for the Dead.

Also the Brotherhood of St. Vincent of Paul for visiting and relieving the poor; and the Ladies' Charitable Society for visiting poor females, &c. The confraternity of the Immaculate Heart of Mary have lately procured from Munich, a beautiful statue of their sweet Patroness carved in wood, and richly painted and gilt.

The Services.

The regular Services at St. George's are weekly announced and affixed to a board near the entrance.

Masses every morning from eight to ten. Evening devotions on Mondays at eight; Wednesdays at eight; Thursdays at half-past seven; Fridays at eight; and Saturdays at eight. The Confessionals are attended regularly on every morning, and on Wednesday, Friday, and Saturday evenings, and the eves of festivals, and on other occasions, as notified. There are several Confraternity masses during the week. On Sundays masses from six to eleven, at which hour the High Mass commences. After the High Mass children are christened. At three catechetical instructions, which are also given during the week. Vespers and Benediction at half-past six, but on holidays at half-past seven.

The Cathedral is open from six in the morning to six in the evening for private devotions. The presence of the Blessed Sacrament, which is always on one of the altars, is indicated by a red light.

The Church is solely supported by the voluntary contributions of the faithful, whose offerings are collected at each service. The only foundation at present is the Petre Chantry, and it is hoped that others will follow the same pious example. There are also many portions of the Cathedral unfinished from the want of funds, such as particularly, the *Tower*, the want of which is very striking from whatever point the Cathedral is approached ; *the decoration of the Chancel*, which looks very bare between the two richly decorated chapels ; *the colouring and partial gilding of the roofs*, which would very greatly relieve their present heavy appearance; a *sounding board* and canopy for the pulpit, and a *lofty cover* for the font ; a *fixed episcopal throne* for the chancel ; these and some other decorative portions it is hoped some pious and zealous persons will be moved to contribute, and thus render St. George's one of the most perfect Cathedrals in the kingdom.

THE BENEDICTINE SOLITARIES of the Perpetual Adoration, established in the London Road, humbly entreat the continuance of the kind aid bestowed on them, especially in the purchase of the artificial flowers and other fancy works made by the nuns ; their order being laborious, not mendicant.

STRANGER'S GUIDE TO THE SITUATION OF THE
CATHOLIC CHURCHES AND CHAPELS
IN LONDON AND VICINITY, 1851.

THE CITY.
* Moorfields, Bloomfield Street.
Cheapside, Great St. Thomas Apostle, KIRCHE DEUTSCH.

EASTWARD.
* Bunhill Row, Lamb's Buildings, (temporary.)
Hackney, the Triangle.
Ratclif Highway, Virginia St.
* Commercial Road East, Lucas Street.
* Spitalfields, Spicer Street, (temporary.)

CENTRAL.
* Lincoln's Inn Fields, Duke St. CHIESA ITALIANA.
* Clerkenwell, Upper Rosamond Street.
* Soho Square, Sutton Street.
* Charing Cross, King William Street.

WESTWARD.
* Regent Street, Warwick Street.
* Manchester Square, Spanish Place.
* Portman Square, Little George Street, EGLISE FRANÇAISE.
* Berkeley Square, Farm Street.
Westminster, Romney Terrace.

WESTERN VICINITY.
* Chelsea, Cadogan Terrace.
Kensington, Holland Street.
* Hammersmith, King Street.

Turnham Green.
Fulham Fields.

NORTHERN VICINITY.
* St. John's Wood, Grove Road.
The Hyde.
* Hampstead, Holly Place.
Kentish Town, Fitzroy Terrace.
* Somers Town, Clarendon Square.
* Islington, Duncan Terrace.

EASTERN VICINITY.
* Poplar, Wade Street.
* Bermondsey, Dockhead.
Tottenham, Chapel Place.

SOUTHERN VICINITY.
* Southwark, St. George's Road.
London Bridge, Webb St., (temporary.)
* Clapham, Clapham Park Road.
Greenwich, Croom's Hill.
Deptford, by the Station.
Woolwich, New Road.

Two or more Low Masses are said generally from 7 to 10, in the Churches marked thus, * before the High Mass at 11; in the others there is but one or two Masses on the Sunday, the last being always at 11.

For further information, we refer the reader to the "Catholic Directory for 1851," to be had of any Catholic bookseller.